Surviving in a Deserted Island

Jang Geon

Jang Geon

ISBN: 9798608683510

CONTENTS

1. Desolate Island

A cruise ship named '*Argon*' was going to Los Angeles. There were about fifty people on board. The five young passengers named Evan Jason, Gil Oscar, Roka Kim, Jaka Robert, Stella White met at the swimming pool party on the little cruise ship. The five children became very close to each other. They stayed in the same room during the voyage and had a great time chatting and playing.

But suddenly, the huge tidal waves and the cyclones came, and the ship broke into two parts and flew away.

The passengers all washed away by the big wave or drowned to death.

Four children swept away onto an uninhabited island without a name. They all lost their minds.

When they came to their senses, they saw the ship that was split into two. They went into the broken ship and fumbled around for some useful things or food box. There was no food and no useful things, like kinds of firewood, harpoons, guns, hunting bows... They got out disappointedly.

They found a shell on the sand and they began to examine the soil of the island.

2. Hell

A hard, rough, stiff grass covered the ground of the island.

Stella and Jaka set out in search of a shelter. Evan and Gil searched for something to eat. Then suddenly, an unknown wild animal came out.

Evan and Gil started running recklessly and fell off the cliff.

Evan came to his senses and found himself in the entrance to a cave under the cliff. A stream flowed gently down in front of the cave entrance.

He also found Gil had fainted away next to him. Evan was about to wake him up, but Gil regained consciousness by himself. Gil had a pain in his left leg and he couldn't walk by himself. He couldn't help leaning on Evan.

They saw a dim light from the cave. They stepped carefully deep into the cave. The deeper they went, the brighter it was. They faced a two-carved tunnels and they didn't know which way they had to go. So Evan picked up two small stones from the floor and threw them into each tunnel. A thud sound came from the right tunnel as though it struck against the wall. They decided to go into the right tunnel. The tunnel looked brighter than the left tunnel. When they reached the middle of the right tunnel, it got dark.

Suddenly, they heard noisy sound. It sounded like people were chatting. They were coming toward them. They froze and got goose pimples on their bodies. The figures were Stella and Jaka.

"Hey, Stella, Jake, how did you come here?" asked Evan.

"Is there another entrance to this cave?" asked Gil.

"There is an entrance over there," replied Stella, pointing the way she came from.

"Where on earth did you come from?" added Stella.

"Hey, Gil, what happened to your leg?" asked Jake.

"We ran away from a terrible beast and fell off the cliff into the entrance to this cave," answered Gil.

"Oh, I see, there are two entrances to this cave, this way and that way," said Jaka.

Evan thought that the cave would be their proper shelter connecting their camp to the stream.
They came out of the cave and built a camp right in front of the cave he passed through.

3. Safe House

They needed to build a safe house. But no one knew how to build a house. Suddenly Gil said, "I have ever seen some people building a strong base camp using steel plates, fabrics, branches, etc. on TV."

And then, Evan exclaimed, ``okay! We can do it! First, let's go out to find the building materials."

Evan was in charge of wood, Jaka and Stella took off the scrap metal of the broken ship, and Gil got some fabric from the cabin on the ship. About two hours later, they all came to the camp with some materials.

Gil happily trimmed the wood with a pocket knife and made a wooden hammer. Stella and Jaka quickly made a wooden box and stored their materials in it. Gil also made two thin wooden needles, gave them to Stella and Jaka, and told them to sew all the cloth. Evan and Gil built the framework of the house out of the wood. Gil then slightly filled the sides with steel plates removed from the ship. He gave Evan his pocket knife and asked him to make the 28 wooden posts and sharpen one end of each post. And then they tied the posts together with the rope made by Jaka and Stella.

A perfect barricade was completed and they put it up around the house.

They placed other wooden posts on the top of the frame and covered it with the huge cloth that Stella and Jaka sew.

4. The Law of Survival

After making their safe nest, they noticed something flickering at the shore. They rushed toward it and Gil picked it up. It was covered with seaweed. It looked like a radio. He took the seaweed away and pushed the red button.

Suddenly the radio worked and Roka's voice came out of it. He sounded like he was asking for help in an emergency.

"zzzzz.... If there's anyone there, please... save me....zzzzz."

Gil pressed the send button.

"Is that Roka? If you get it, build a fire and give off smoke, and we will find you," said Gil.

A few minutes later, they saw smoke rising from the east. It was one kilometer away from the island.

"What is happening to Roca?" asked Stanla.

"I'm not sure, but he might be in danger," said Evan.

"Let's go rescue him right now!" suggested Jaka.

Gil and Evan headed toward the smoke on a raft. They stepped on the sandy beach where Roka had been limping.

"Roka! Are you all right?" cried Gil.

"Gil, Evan! Thank you, thank you for coming to me," cried Roka. They gave each other a big hug and sobbed.

"This is filled with weird wild animals and I was almost eaten by them. We have to get out of here in a hurry," added Roka.

"Oh! We can't be their food. Hurry up! Let's go to our safe nest," suggested Evan. They jumped on the raft and went back to the island where their new nest was.

When they arrived at the nest, Stanla and Jaka served roasted fish. But it was not enough for them all.

"This island is lack of food," complained Stanla.

'"There are pigs, wild chickens and wild cows on that island. Yes, this island seems to have a lot of wood," said Roka.

"I have a good idea! How about building a huge ship out of a lot of wood," suggested Gil.

"So that we can go to the island to get the food," added Gil.

"Oh, what a good idea!" agreed Evan.

"Let's make it right now!" said Jaka.

"But we don't know how to make a ship," worried Stanla.

"I have built a ship model in ship museum," said Gil.

"Ok, what shall we do first?" asked Stanla.

"First, let's eat it, I'm so hungry!" said Gil.

After eating, they started to gather timbers.

5. Hunting and Survival

Gil gave Evan a stone axe and a stringy rope, and he asked him to bring in about 80 timbers.

"About 80 timbers? I think we need only 30 trees," grumbled Evan. He quickly ran into the woods. Soon big thuds came out of the woods.

Evan came back to the tent at around 6 a.m. the next morning. The amount of wood he cut down was really huge. Evan worked so hard that he couldn't stand up.

Eventually Evan collapsed and Gil carried him into a tent. Gil made a plan for making a ship on a wooden plank.

`'"Let's start to make it tomorrow because we're too tired today,"' Gil said.

"Okay, Evan can't move now either," agreed Roka.

So their work was postponed to the next day.

6. Food Problems

They completed the ship but were suffering from food problems. Roka caught a fish, but it was not enough for them all. Roka and Evan already seemed to faint from hunger.

"Let me go and find some herbs or mushrooms!" said Stanla. Soon Stanla left and roamed the woods in search of something to eat.

Finally she spotted a tree with some fruits like coconuts. The tree was very tall. She tried to climb it to pick the fruits. She managed to climb the tree and reach the fruits. She picked 10 fruits and started to climb down. But she lost balance and fell to the ground. She got injured in the arms and legs.

She used all her energy to go back to their camp. As soon as she arrived there, she fell with a thud.

7. Stanla's Injury

Stanla was bleeding terribly. She couldn't move.

"Stanla, are you ok?" asked Gil. Stanla didn't say and just growled.

"We need to sterilize his wound," Evan said anxiously.

Evan rushed to the beach and scooped up seawater with a coconut shell. He boiled the water and cooled it. And then, he sprayed it around Stanla's wound.

Gil took a piece of cloth and put it around her hurt arm and leg.

It has been two days since Stanla was injured. The fruits that Stanla brought with her powered them up a little bit. Stanla was still suffering from the wound.

"Let's go catch some fish to feed Stanla," suggested Roka.

"Good idea! Let me stay and take care of Stanla," said Gil.

The three boys went to the beach and tried to catch fish. Luckily, they caught about 10 fish.

"How about making fish porridge for Stanla?" suggested Evan.

"Do you know how to make it?" asked Roka.

"Sure, I have ever cooked chicken porridge," boasted Roka.

"Okay, tell us what we need to make the fish porridge," said Evan.

Roka asked for some fish fillet, some whole wheat flour, some water, and some salt. He asked for the container like a saucepan. They all went back to their camp and tried to make the porridge. Roka muttered the recipe.

Pour 2 cups of water and boil it.
Stir-fry whole wheat flour in a thick saucepan until it's golden,
stir-fry it well, stir-fry it well,
and then boil the ingredients all slowly,
and then add some salt to it,
put it in a bowl, and enjoy it.

They finished making the fish porridge and fed Stanla. And then they all shared the porridge.

"Thanks a lot for making this porridge for me. After eating, I feel much better," Stanla said smiling.

"It's a good thing you enjoy it and feel better," said Roka.

8. Escape Plan

Evan and his friends were determined to get out of this sickly island. Evan, Gil and Roka decided to go into the tunnel on the left in the cave which they had never been to before.

"'I'll go with you and we'll need this stuff," said Roka. Then as if waiting, Gil asked, "what are you holding in your hand?"

"It's a fluorescent lamp," said Roka.

"I made it by myself," added Roka.

"How did you make it?" asked Gil.

"It is from a highlighter in a warehouse on an abandoned half-broken cruise," said Roka,

"I picked it up, cut off the back, put the fluorescent material inside into an empty PET bottle of water and then diluted it in a little water," explained Roka.

After that, Evan and Gil immediately went to the warehouse of the abandoned ship and brought two highlighters and another PET bottle. Then they made another fluorescent lamp and took the string and hook that Evan picked up when he went to the warehouse. And then, they went into the left tunnel in the cave and kept walking forward.

When the three boys went into the cave, the two girls went to the beach to pick up crabs, marsh snails. At the back of the left tunnel, the boys found another deep cave and wondered what was in it. So Roka threw a fluorescent light and they looked down. There was a very large lightplane.

The children were surprised and hurried to tell the girls.

Jaka and Stanla saw Gil, Evan, and Roka running hurriedly.

`''Why are you running? Did you see any planes?'' asked Stanla.

Gil, Evan and Roka asked again in surprise, "how did you know?" Stanla shouted for joy at the moment. And then they started thinking about how to get the plane up.

Roka suggested making a pulley and lifting the plane with it. And then they went to the half-broken ship and picked up some stuff for making a pulley.

9. Test-fly of a Five-seat light plane

They pulled up the plane with the pulley as they planned and figured out what the problem was. Evan and Gil looked at the plane carefully and found out that it ran out of fuel.

The left wing of the plane was broken, so the plane was out of balance. They fixed it with the rope and wooden planks. After that, they got an empty bucket of gasoline from the tunnel where the plane was abandoned. On the top of the bucket, there was a piece of paper that looked like a map. Evan looked carefully at the map and saw the picture of fuel on the map.

"Wow, it must be located on top of the mountain on this island," Gil shouted pointing at the fuel picture.

They carried the plane to their camp, and then went up to the top of the mountain. There were real fuel cans buried in the ground.

But lots of oil had spilled out of most of the fuel barrels. When they came back with all the fuel cans, there were a little left in each barrel. It was for only about 8 hours of flying time. Anyway, they cleaned the plane hard.

All of the kids wanted to test-fly the plane. But they were so scared of it. But they tried hard to steer the plane as soon as possible. Finally, they found out how to use the engine and how to roll the wheels below. Then they flattened the side of the mountain and made a runway. They made a fuel rank out of wood. And then they gathered all the pieces of glass in the light airplane, melted them and made three convex lenses. After that, they combined the three lenses to make a telescope. They could see other islands with the telescope. They also remodeled the plane to load their luggage onto it.

The light plane could carry up to 500 kilograms, the manual said.

10. Goodbye, Desolate island

From dawn, they were so busy preparing for escaping the dreaded desolate island. They went to the waterfall to fill the barrel with water. But there, Evan tripped by mistake and fell into the waterfall, where he found a cave that went down.

Evan shouted, "hey! Gil, come here with a lamp."

Gil took the lamp there and shone it around the cave. There were some brilliant minerals in the cave.

Gil stared at them with his mouth open. And then they looked each other in the eye silently and nodded at each other. As soon as they came out, they began to make pickaxes. They made a good team for the treasure.

Before long, the pickaxes were made out of long stones and sharp stones. They began to dig up the ores. There were various ores. In addition, they dug up about 8 kilograms of diamonds. Soon they took the diamond outside. Then Roka, Stanla and Jaka opened their eyes wide and shouted, `"wow!!!! Where did you find these diamonds?"

"We found a cave under the waterfall and we saw lots of ores there," answered Evan.

After that they were all ready to leave the uninhabited island.

They all boarded the plane with excitement. And Evan and Gil who test-flew the most were supposed to fly the plane. They slowly turned on the power switch, ran the engine as described in the manual, turned on the front winged motor, and stepped on the accelerator. Then the plane was running toward the cliff. Then Gil and Evan flew the plane into the sky, holding on to the steering wheel.

"At last, we got out of this disgusting island!" exclaimed Jaka. They all took a sip of the drinking water from the barrel and tried to find another island where they newly settle down while flying.

After six hours of flying, an island finally caught their eyes. They landed on the flat land of the island. Fortunately, it was the island where people reside.

"It's not desolate island! Thanks god!" exclaimed Gil.

Epilogue

Three years have passed since the five kids escaped from the desolate island. They converted the jewels they had taken from the island into money.

High-quality diamonds could fetch quite a price. They each got a small house on the new island, and also built a theme park on the uninhabited island where they escaped from with their money.

And Gil, who was good at anything, wrote a book about the uninhabited island and their survival.

The book and the 'Surviving in a Deserted Island' theme park became more and more popular. Many people all over the world visit the theme park.

They earned more and more money and became more and more famous. They got into papaers and were on TV. Their families noticed them and visited the theme park. And they lived happily ever after, managing the theme park.

About the Author

Hello, I am Jang Gun who wrote ***Surviving in a Deserted Island.***

I am a 14 year-old-boy and live in Ulsan, South Korea.

Before I wrote this book, I was interested in uninhabited islands. It was also fun to write down each of the survival methods.

Finally, I had a chance to write this book. That's why I wrote this story.

I hope you enjoy it.

www.ingramcontent.com/pod-product-compliance
Lightning Source LLC
Chambersburg PA
CBHW051339150726
47997CB00004B/1529